This book is to be returned on or before
the last date stamped below.

D0512845

Pearson Education Limited
Edinburgh Gate, Harlow,
Essex CM20 2JE, England
and Associated Companies throughout the world.

ISBN 0 582 41979 4

First published as *The Children* by Michael Joseph 1959
This edition first published 2000

5 7 9 10 8 6 4

Typeset by Ferdinand Pageworks, London
Set in 11/14pt Bembo
Printed in Spain by Mateu Cromo, S. A. Pinto (Madrid)

Published by Pearson Education Limited in association with
Penguin Books Ltd, both companies being subsidiaries of Pearson Plc

Contents

Introduction

The bush boy walked alone. He was on his walkabout. He had to live in the desert alone for six months. He had to find food and water. He had to kill animals, and find fruit on the trees.

In Australia, when an Aboriginal man-child is sixteen, his tribe sends him out into the Australian Bush. A lot of the bush is desert. The bush boy has to live there alone for months. The Aboriginals call this time the 'walkabout'.

This is the story of an Aboriginal boy's walkabout, but it is also the story of two American children. Mary and Peter are lost in the Australian desert after an aeroplane crash. Their uncle is waiting for them in Adelaide, a long way away. The desert is a strange world for the children. They come from a city, and things are different there. When they meet the bush boy, they learn about the desert. They also start to think about their world. But can the story end happily for the three children?

James Vance Marshall (Donald Payne) is the writer of this story and of a number of other books. You can read them in fifteen different languages, and three are now films. The book and the film of *Walkabout* are very famous.

Australian Birds and Animals

kookaburra

wombat

dingo

cockatoo

wallaby

bustard

marsupial tiger cat

koala

Chapter 1   Lost in the Australian Bush

The aeroplane crashed in the middle of nowhere. There were no roads, no houses and no people. There was only bush, and rocks as far as the eyes could see. Only two children survived the crash.

The aeroplane was on fire. The girl pulled her small brother away from it.

'Run, Pete,' she shouted. 'Quick!'

They ran through the bush as fast as they could. Then they started to climb up through some rocks. Near the top, they stopped and looked down. From the rocks, they watched the fire.

'Where are we?' asked Peter.

The girl didn't answer. She didn't know. They were lost in the Australian desert. But she couldn't tell Peter that.

♦

Twenty-five hundred kilometres away, in the big city of Adelaide, Uncle Keith was at the airport. He looked at his watch. Keith's brother worked in America. He lived in Charleston, South Carolina, with his wife and two children. This was the children's first visit to Australia. But their aeroplane was late. It was *very* late. Uncle Keith waited and waited. He talked to other families. They asked about the plane, but nobody at the airport could tell them anything. Then people began to talk about an accident, about a plane crash. There were no survivors.

♦

Now it was dark, and the children were alone. They were cold, so they climbed down between some rocks. They could see nothing, they could hear nothing. They were lost, and they were afraid.

The aeroplane crashed in the middle of nowhere.

'It's all right, Peter,' said Mary.

His sister's arms were round him. That felt better. When a boy is only eight, a big sister of thirteen can be wonderful.

They talked quietly, perhaps because there was no other noise. Or perhaps because they were afraid.

'Mary,' Peter said, 'I'm hungry. Have you got any chocolate?'

Mary found the chocolate. She broke it in two, and gave half to him. They sat very quietly in the black night. Then Peter started to move again.

'My leg hurts,' he said. Mary looked at it.

'It's all right,' she said. 'It'll be better in the morning.'

Peter was quiet again. He fell asleep with Mary's arms round him. But Mary couldn't sleep. She watched her young brother. She was sister and mother to him now. She thought about the aeroplane journey and the accident, and she thought about her mother and her father. But her head felt heavy. Then she was asleep too.

In the dark, the animals in the bush began to move. A wombat walked round the children. He pushed them with his nose, but he wasn't dangerous. He was interested in these strange new desert animals, but he didn't want to eat them. He only ate plants. Birds and insects started to fly round in the sky. A big marsupial tiger cat came near and looked at the children. She looked for a minute or two, but these strange animals were very big. Her young babies couldn't eat them! So she walked quietly away.

In the east, the sky was grey. It was the beginning of another day. Then the sun came up. It brought new colours to the bush: greens and whites and reds and yellows. Many people think that the desert is one boring colour. They think there are no plants. But here in the Australian desert there were beautiful plants in many different colours.

The children slept through the wonderful early morning. A large grey bird, a kookaburra, sat in a tree above the children. He wanted food – a small animal, or some insects. But on the rocks below him, he could see only two very large animals. They were different from the other desert animals. He wanted to tell every animal and bird in the desert about them. He opened his mouth and made a loud noise. It wasn't a song, because the kookaburra doesn't sing.

The girl opened her eyes and looked up. She was afraid, but then she saw the bird. So it was only a bird! She laughed, and looked at Peter. Good! He was asleep. He couldn't hear the bird. Peter looked small and thin and very, very young. She loved him very much.

'When he wakes up, he'll be hungry. What can I give him?' she thought.

There was more chocolate, but there wasn't very much. And that was all. She got up and looked round. Down below her she could see a small river, so water wasn't a problem. But how could they find food? What could they eat? People died without food. She looked at the kookaburra. He made another loud noise.

'Not me,' he said. Then he flew away, up into the sky.

There were other birds – big, white cockatoos in the trees, and smaller birds near the river, on the rocks and in the water. They played happily.

Mary felt hot, and her dress was dirty. She wanted to go down there and swim with them. She looked round her. Peter was asleep. There were no other people there in the bush with them. Nobody could see her. She undressed and went down to the river. The green water was wonderful and clean. She laughed and played. She swam under the water, so the birds could see only her long hair. She was happy again.

It was now warm and sunny and light. Her brother heard the sound of water and opened his eyes.

'Where am I?' For a minute, he was lost. He wasn't in his bedroom. He wasn't in an aeroplane. Then he saw Mary in the river.

The green water was wonderful and clean.

'Hi, Mary!' he shouted. 'I'm coming too.'

He climbed down to the river quickly. He threw off his clothes and jumped off a rock into the middle of the river.

'Peter! What are you doing? You can't swim!'

She swam to him and pulled him to the rocks. There she helped him out of the water.

'I can, I can! I can swim,' he said.

'OK,' she said. 'But not in the middle. Stay near the rocks.'

He jumped into the river again, but this time he stayed near the rocks. Mary watched him for a minute. Then she remembered. She had no clothes on. She got out of the river on to the rocks and put her dress on quickly. Peter looked up at her.

'Your dress is wet,' he said. 'Why didn't you get dry first?'

'Come out now, Peter, and put your clothes on.'

Mary pulled him out of the water, and dried him with his shirt. Then she helped him dress. He was happy after his swim.

'I'm hungry,' he said. 'What can we eat?'

'Here's some chocolate.'

Mary gave the chocolate to him. Peter looked at it.

'It's very small. Is that all?'

'Yes, that's all,' said Mary sadly.

Peter ate the chocolate quickly, and then he ran away from her. He started to play in the rocks.

'He doesn't understand the problems. That's good,' thought Mary. But there were a lot of questions in her head. What can we do next? Where can we go? How can we find Uncle Keith? She had no answers.

'Mary! Mary!' Peter shouted. 'Come quickly!'

She climbed over the rocks to him. His hands were inside his jeans.

'Something's hurting me,' he cried.

Mary pulled down Peter's jeans and looked at his legs. There were a lot of insects all over them, and there were more insects on the ground. His legs were very red.

'It's all right,' she said. 'They're only ants.'

'My legs really hurt!' he cried.

She pushed him away from the insects.

'OK, Peter. Now, sit down.'

She pulled off his trousers, and hit the ants on his legs.

'Ow,' he cried loudly. But the insects went away quickly.

'There aren't any ants now, Pete. It's all right.'

Peter looked at his legs. They were very red, and they hurt. He started to cry. Mary put her arms round him and he felt better. He stopped crying for a minute, but then he started again.

'What is it, Pete?'

'I don't like this place, Mary. I want to go home.'

'We can't go home, Pete. Home is in America. How can we get across the sea?'

'Then let's go to Uncle Keith's. In Adelaide.'

Mary looked at him. 'So you remember!' she said. 'All right, I'll take you to Uncle Keith.'

He stopped crying.

'When? Now?'

'Yes,' she said, 'now. We'll walk to Adelaide now.'

Mary was only thirteen, but she was clever. Adelaide was in the south of Australia. It was early morning and the sun was on her left. The sun was in the east in the morning, so south was in front of them. The small river in front of them also went south.

'Let's go, Peter,' she said to her brother.

They started to walk down the river.

♦

For the first half an hour, it was easy and Peter walked fast. Then it got harder. There were big plants in front of them. They climbed over them, or they walked round them. After two hours,

Pete was tired. Walking was difficult. He didn't say anything, but Mary knew.

'Let's sit down here,' she said.

He sat near her, and put his head in his hands. They said nothing. They watched the river.

'I'm hungry, Mary. What are we going to eat?'

'Oh Peter! It's not lunch-time!'

'When will it be lunch-time?'

'I'll tell you.'

But there were more questions.

'What are we going to eat for lunch?'

'We'll find something.'

But what could they find? There were a lot of plants, but they didn't have any food on them. Quickly, Mary got up.

'All right. Let's find some food.'

Peter jumped up.

'Great idea!' he said.

They looked in the river, but they couldn't find any fish. The fish were asleep at the bottom of the river. They looked in the trees for birds, but birds in the Australian desert sleep in the day. They looked in the bush for animals, but the animals were asleep in the rocks. They didn't find any food.

'I don't like this game,' said Peter. 'I want to go home.'

They walked and walked. They were hungry and tired. Then the bush was more open, and they could see better. There was high ground in front of them.

'Mary!'

'Yes, Pete?'

'Look up there! Let's climb to the top. Perhaps we'll see the sea.'

'That's a good idea.'

They started to climb. They climbed for four and a half hours and then they arrived at the top. The desert to the south in front of them was beautiful. The light of the evening sun was

The desert to the south in front of them was beautiful.

wonderful. And there, far away, they could see water. It shone in the evening sun. The boy danced happily.

'Look, Mary. Look! The sea. The sea. It isn't far. Look!'

'Don't look, Pete,' she said quietly. She put her arms round the little boy. 'I'm very, very sorry.'

It wasn't water. Mary knew that. It was the Great Australian Desert. Hundreds of kilometres of it.

'We can't walk to the sea today, Pete. Let's find a place for the night,' said Mary sadly. She got up and pulled Peter to his feet. 'We'll walk to the sea tomorrow. Tomorrow we won't be hungry.'

Chapter 2   A Meeting with a Bush Boy

The next morning, Mary woke up first. She looked up at the birds in the sky. Then Peter woke up too.

'Mary, let's go! Let's walk to the sea.'

'First we have to look for food,' said Mary. 'We have to take some food with us on our journey.'

'Good idea!' said Peter. 'I'm *very* hungry.'

They looked and looked for food. For a long time they found nothing. Then Peter shouted:

'Look, Mary! Fruit.'

There was a tree with round balls of fruit on it. Some of the balls were green, and some were red. Mary thought carefully for a minute. You could get ill from some fruits. But they had to eat. She ran to the tree. She ate a green fruit and it was good. Then she ate a red fruit – it was better.

'Try these, Peter. They're nicer.'

The children ate and ate.

'That's good!' said Peter. 'I'm not thirsty now. We don't have to carry water. We can take some of these with us.'

Mary pulled her skirt up in front of her. She took some fruit and put it there. Peter began to find more fruit too. He went from tree to tree.

'Mary! Somebody's here,' he called back to her.

'Don't be stupid, Peter.'

'I'm not stupid! Somebody's watching us.'

Mary turned round. Her mouth fell open, and she put her hand up to her face. There was a boy very near them, only a metre away. He was black, and he was naked. Mary started to run away, but then she looked again. The boy was young, and friendly. He smiled, so perhaps he wasn't dangerous. At home in South Carolina, there were black Africans. But this boy was browner, and his hair was different. He had big blue-black eyes, and he had a baby wallaby in one hand.

Peter and Mary looked at the boy for a long time, and he looked at them. Nobody spoke, and nobody moved. They waited and waited. They were from different worlds. Peter and Mary came from a big city. There, people looked after them. The bush boy lived in the desert. It was his home, and he understood it. The bush boy put the wallaby on the ground. It was dead. He smiled.

'*Worumgala*?' (Where do you come from?)

Mary looked at Peter, and Peter looked at Mary. They didn't understand. The bush boy tried again.

'*Worum mwa*?' (Where are you going?)

'We don't understand you, boy,' said Peter. 'But we're lost. Show us the way to Adelaide. Uncle Keith lives there. Which way do we go?'

The black boy smiled again, and Peter smiled back. The boy went to Peter and felt his face. Then he put his hand on Peter's hair. Then he felt his clothes – the shirt, and the jeans.

'Those are trousers, boy. Why haven't *you* got any? You're naked! It's not right. Aren't there any shops here?'

But the bush boy was too busy. He didn't listen. He looked at Peter's shoes. Then he turned to Mary.

Mary wasn't very happy. At home in Charleston, South Carolina, no black person came near white people. But a lot of people in Charleston had strange ideas, and this boy didn't look dangerous. So it was OK. She didn't move.

The bush boy felt her face, and her arms too. And he felt her clothes. Then he looked at her carefully for a long time. Mary waited. 'He'll finish, and then he'll go away,' she thought.

Peter waited too. First he waited quietly, and watched the bush boy. Then he began to kick the ground with his feet. Suddenly his face changed colour. It went very red. He put his hand to his nose. He shut his mouth, and he made a strange noise. Mary turned round.

'Peter, what *are* you doing?' asked Mary.

Peter put his face in his hands. But nothing could stop him now. Suddenly there was a loud noise. Peter sneezed! And then he sneezed again, very, very loudly.

'Stop it, Peter!' said Mary. She was angry because she wasn't in charge now. Behind her, there was a different noise. The bush boy laughed. He laughed because Peter's sneeze was a very big sneeze from a very small boy. Then Peter laughed too. The two boys fell to the ground. They kicked their legs and moved their arms. They couldn't stop. They laughed and laughed.

Mary watched them. She wanted to laugh too, but she was too old for that. So she went to Peter.

'Stop that, now, Peter.'

Peter sat up and looked at her. The bush boy looked at her too. Slowly he got up, and walked back to his wallaby. He took it, and walked quietly away. He went down the hill. Then he went behind some trees and they couldn't see him.

'Mary!' Peter cried. 'What did you do? Look! He's going!'

Mary was quiet. She was afraid of the bush boy, because he was naked. And she didn't want help from him. It was wrong. At home in South Carolina, you didn't ask a black boy for help. But he was the only person there, and perhaps he *could* help them.

Peter was younger, and life was easier for him. He liked the bush boy, and they had to have help. He jumped up and down.

'Mary, let's go after him. Let's find him.'

He ran quickly through the bush.

'Peter! Wait!' Mary called after him.

But Peter didn't stop.

'Hey, boy!' he shouted. 'We're coming too. Wait for us! Wait for us!'

The bush boy turned and waited.

'Hey, don't leave us!' said Peter. 'We want food, and drink. And Adelaide! Where's Adelaide?'

The black boy didn't understand, but he laughed. Peter tried again.

'Look, boy, we're lost. We want water. Do you understand water? WA–TER. WA–TER.'

He made a cup with his hands, and took them up to his mouth. The bush boy understood now. He didn't laugh this time. In the bush people were often thirsty. He made a cup with his hands too.

'*Arkooloola*,' he said.

'That's it, boy. You understand! *Arkooloola*. We want *arkooloola*. And food too.'

He put his hand to his face, and moved his mouth.

'*Yeemara*,' said the bush boy.

'Yes! That's right. We want *yeemara* and a*rkooloola*. But where can we find them?'

The black boy turned and walked into the bush. Then he stopped and looked back.

'*Kurura*,' he said.

'Let's go,' the boy called out to Mary. '*Kurura*, that means "follow me".'

And he ran after the bush boy.

'Kurura,' *he said.*

Chapter 3   Life in the Bush

The bush boy walked for about an hour, and the children followed. Then they came to some very tall trees. After the strong sun in the open bush, it was quite dark. Mary and Peter couldn't see very well, and they fell again and again. But it was quiet, and nothing moved. And it wasn't as hot as the desert. The bush boy walked quickly.

Hour after hour the bush boy walked, and Mary and Peter followed. The bush boy never got tired, but Peter did.

'Wait for me, Mary. You're walking too fast!'

Mary stopped.

'All right, Pete,' she said to her little brother, 'it'll be all right. We'll wait for you.'

'My legs hurt!'

'Here, Pete. Take my hand.'

She was happy, because now she was his big sister again. Peter pulled on her hand.

'I'm thirsty! I'm hungry!'

'Me too, Pete.' Her mouth was hot and dry. 'But we can't stop now.'

Suddenly the trees ended, and there was the desert again, kilometres and kilometres of desert, with its hot, hot sun and no water.

'*Kurura*!' said the bush boy.

He left the trees and started to walk in the desert. But Mary stopped.

'Where's the food? Where's the water? It's too far for us. We'll never find it.'

She sat down under the last tree before the desert, and Peter sat down next to her. The bush boy came back. He spoke quietly, in his strange language. But they understood.

'You have to follow me, or you'll die. There's water. It's not far now. Look over there!'

With his hand, he showed them some rocks and a small hill.

'But that's a long way,' said Mary. The desert was hot, but here under the trees it was nice. It was easier to stay here. And was the bush boy right? Was there *really* water in those rocks in the middle of the desert?

'*Arkooloola*,' the bush boy said, again and again.

Mary looked harder. It was dark round the bottom of the hill. Why? Were there bushes? Green trees and bushes?

'There *is* water there, Pete! Trees are only as green as that when there's water!'

She jumped up, and the three children walked out into the desert.

♦

The sun went down before they arrived at the hill. But there was a little light and they could see the green bushes. They walked through them.

'*Arkooloola*,' said the bush boy, and smiled.

Mary and Peter were excited. They could hear water. It was very near. Peter wasn't tired now, and he ran in front of them.

'It's water, Mary! Water,' he shouted.

'*Arkooloola*,' said the bush boy again.

Peter was on the ground, with his head in beautiful, clean water. Mary sat down on the ground next to him, and the two white children drank. They drank and drank. The water was good, but it was warm. The bush boy sat next to Mary. With his hands he took water from the bottom of the river. Mary did the same. Now the water was colder and better.

The bush boy drank only a little. Then he stood up. He climbed up the hill and sat on a rock. He was interested in the children. He watched them carefully. They were strange. They

16

'Trees are only as green as that when there's water!'

didn't know the desert. They didn't know anything. Where were they from? Why were they here? They couldn't live alone in the desert.

'I have to help them,' he thought.

The small boy stopped drinking, and climbed up to the bush boy. The rocks were big, and it was difficult for him. The bush boy put out his hand and helped him up. Peter sat down and looked at the wallaby. He felt it with his hands.

'Eat?' he asked. '*Yeemara*?'

The bush boy smiled, and got up. He climbed down from the rocks. He looked at different rocks, and stopped in front of a big flat piece. Then he found some wood. Peter watched, but he didn't understand.

'*Larana*,' said the bush boy.

He began to build a fire.

'I know!' Peter was excited. 'Fire. You're going to make a fire.'

'*Larana*,' said the bush boy again.

'OK. *Larana*. You're going to make a *larana*. I'll help.'

The bush boy found more wood and Peter helped him. But Peter stopped suddenly.

'How can we light a fire,' he asked, 'when we haven't got any . . .?'

Peter didn't finish his question, but watched the bush boy with his mouth open. Australian trees have very dry wood, and Aboriginals can make fire in the old way. The bush boy sat by the flat rock. He put some very small pieces of wood on the rock. Then he took a long piece of wood between his hands. He put the end of this into the small pieces, and moved it round and round very fast. And very quickly, there was a good fire.

'That's clever!' said Peter. He put some more wood on the fire.

Mary sat alone and watched the boys. Peter followed the bush boy everywhere. He didn't want her now. Boys didn't want to be with girls.

'Why can't I be a boy too?' she thought. She watched the smoke from the fire sadly.

The boy took the wallaby, and cooked it slowly on the fire. An hour later, they sat down near the fire and ate it. A dingo sat on a rock only ten metres away, and watched them. There was a lot of meat, and they ate it all. There wasn't any meat for the dingo.

Now they were tired. The bush boy put some water on the fire. Then the three children slept.

Mary woke up first, before the sun was up. She watched the sky. What was up there? Another life? Life after death? Heaven? She didn't know. She looked at the naked bush boy, and then looked away quickly.

'Why am I not a boy too,' she thought. 'Life is easy for boys.'

She thought about life in the bush with the black boy. He knew the desert, and he could survive. That was good. Then Peter woke up. He sat up and looked at Mary, and then at the bush boy.

'How can we get to Adelaide, Mary? Will the boy take us?'

At home in South Carolina, she usually knew the answers to Peter's questions. But here in the bush, she didn't.

'I don't know,' she said. 'Perhaps he doesn't know Adelaide. And how can we ask him? We don't speak his language.'

There were other questions about the boy in Mary's head too. Why was he alone in the desert? Where was his family? What was best for her and Peter? She didn't have any answers.

'Let's wait and see,' she said to Peter.

'I'm not in charge now,' she thought, and then she felt better. She closed her eyes and fell asleep again.

She woke up after about two hours. Half asleep, she could hear the boys.

'What are you laughing at, Peter?' she called.

But Peter couldn't hear her, so he didn't answer. He shouted and played with the bush boy in the water. Mary sat up and saw the two boys. Peter looked back.

19

'Mary,' he shouted. 'Come here and play with us!'

'Later,' she shouted back. 'When it's warmer!'

Peter ran after the bush boy. They ran round some rocks. Then the bush boy stopped suddenly.

'*Worwora*!' he said, excited.

On the ground, there was a brown ball. It was the top of a plant. Peter felt the brown ball with his hand.

'*Yeemara*?' he asked.

The bush boy smiled. Yes, it was food. He pulled the strange plant out of the ground. The bottom of the plant, *under* the ground was green, and there was also a pretty flower! The bush boy was happy. It was good food. They ran into the desert and looked for other *worwora*.

Mary waited alone. Then she went down to the river. She swam and played in the water. Half an hour later, she heard the boys. They were back. She got out of the water quickly and put on her dress. The boys had twenty or thirty *worwora* in their arms. But now, Peter was naked too!

'Pete, where are your clothes?'

'Oh Mary! Stop being Big Sister! Do this! Do that!'

'Peter,' she said. 'Come here!' She had her brother's trousers in her hands.

'Oh Mary! It's too hot! I don't want any clothes.'

'Put them on,' she said.

Peter wasn't happy, but he went to Mary. He looked at her.

'OK,' he said. 'I'll wear the trousers, but not the shirt.'

◆

Later they found wood and made a fire. The bush boy taught Peter to move the big piece of wood fast on the small pieces. Peter tried very hard. It took a long time, but in the end the fire was red.

'It's easy!' Peter shouted happily.

They cooked the *worwora* and they were very good. Mary watched the black boy. He was clean, and strong. That was good. But why was he naked? Where were his clothes? She didn't understand. Everything was different in her world in South Carolina.

After the food, they felt good. Peter put his hands on his stomach. It was very big now, and he started to laugh. The bush boy laughed, and put his hands on his stomach too. Then he stood up, and started to do an Aboriginal dance. First it was slow, but then it was faster and faster. And then it was stranger and stranger. He danced round and round the fire. Then he stopped in front of Mary. He looked at her, and she looked at him. Nobody moved.

Mary was suddenly afraid, and her eyes were wide open. The bush boy's eyes were wide open too. He wasn't afraid, but for the first time he saw a girl. Mary was a girl, a *lubra*. She wasn't the same as Peter. Then the boy saw something in the girl's eyes. It was dark and strange. She was afraid. To him, that could mean only one thing: the girl saw death, his death.

For the bush boy, and for his tribe, there was a life plan. You were born, and then you walked with your tribe. After that, you walked alone, on your walkabout. Then you were a man, and you lived with a woman. And after that, you died. It never changed. That was life. Now the bush boy walked alone. He was on his walkabout. He had to live in the desert alone for six months. He had to find food and water. He had to kill animals, and find fruit on the trees. Every day was dangerous for him. After his walkabout, he was a man. But the girl could see his death, so there was no future for him. Everything was different for him now.

He stood in the middle of the desert.

'I'm going to die,' he thought.

He was very cold, but he wasn't afraid. Peter looked at the older children.

'Hey, boy! Dance again. I liked that!'

Then he stood up, and started to do an Aboriginal dance.

The other two didn't move. They didn't speak. It was very strange. Peter didn't understand.

'Hey, Mary, what's happening?'

He took Mary's hand, and then he began to cry. The bush boy looked at him. So Peter could see his death too! He turned and slowly walked into the desert. The children watched him. Mary's face was white. Peter was afraid.

'Mary! He's leaving! What'll we do?' he cried. He ran into the desert after the bush boy. 'Hey, boy! Stop! Come back. Come back.'

The bush boy didn't hear, or didn't listen. But Peter ran after him.

'Don't go,' he shouted again.

The bush boy stopped and put his hands on Peter's head. He pushed him away and started to walk again. But Peter followed him.

'Don't go, don't go,' he said again and again.

The bush boy stopped. He turned round and looked at Peter.

'When Peter sees my death in my eyes, he'll run away,' he thought. 'Then I can go.'

But Peter took the bush boy's hand. He looked at him, and smiled.

'That's strange,' thought the bush boy. 'Perhaps I'm not going to die. Perhaps I'm wrong.'

He turned round and looked at Mary.

'Perhaps she's wrong. Perhaps death isn't coming for me now. Perhaps it's on its way to other tribes.'

He walked back to Mary, but she moved away. She *was* afraid. He saw it in her eyes.

'So I *am* going to die,' he thought. 'Perhaps not today, not tomorrow, and not the next day. But before the rains come.'

Chapter 4   The End of the Walkabout

The bush boy thought about the two children. They didn't know the desert and they couldn't find food without him.

'They'll die too,' he thought.

Then he had an idea. He had to take the children to the rivers-under-the-mountains. That was the end of his walkabout, and a good place for them. There was water, and food. There were white people not far from there too. How much time did they have? Not much, perhaps. They had to go quickly. He put out the fire, and took the *worwora* in his arms.

'*Kurura*,' he said.

He walked into the desert. Peter followed, but Mary didn't move. Then she got up.

'Where's he going? I hope he knows,' she thought, and she started to follow too.

They walked in the desert for a long time, up and down, over big rocks and across dry rivers. They went through tall trees and thick plants. It was hot and dirty, but the colours were beautiful – yellows, greens and reds. The bush boy never stopped or looked back. He knew the way.

Then the desert was suddenly more friendly. The trees were taller, and there were a lot of birds and a river. It was midday, and the sun was very hot. The boys drank water from the river with their hands. They put their heads in the water. Mary drank too, but she didn't go near the bush boy. When he looked at her, she looked away.

'What's wrong, Mary?' asked Peter. 'Why are you afraid?'

Mary didn't move, and she didn't say anything.

Peter didn't understand. But Mary was strange sometimes. Girls were often strange. He went to the bush boy, and sat next to him. They ate the *worwora*. Peter gave some to Mary, and she ate them too.

'What's wrong, Mary?'

It was very hot, so they stayed under the trees near the water for three hours. Then the bush boy got up and started to walk again. He usually walked forty-five kilometres in a day, but Peter got tired quickly. So they only walked twenty-five.

On the way, the bush boy killed a big bustard and they ate it for dinner. Then they felt sleepy. That night it was cold, but the rocks stayed warm from the sun. So each child found a big flat rock. But Mary couldn't sleep.

'Peter!'

'Yes?'

'Come and sleep next to me. Please.'

'Why?'

'I'm cold.'

'OK.'

He fell asleep next to her, but Mary watched the bush boy.

'I won't close my eyes. I'll watch him all night,' she thought.

But she was very tired, and of course she fell asleep.

The bush boy didn't sleep. Hour after hour he stood there, on the rocks. He looked out at the desert. He didn't move, and he didn't make any noise.

♦

The children walked the next day, and the next day, and the day after that. They stopped for three hours at midday when the sun was very hot. They found food – plants, fish and small animals. They made fires, and cooked their food. They swam in rivers, and they slept on rocks, or under trees. Peter talked to the bush boy. He learnt more of the bush boy's language. He showed him a rock.

'What do you call this?' he asked.

'*Garsha*,' answered the bush boy.

'*Garsha, garsha*,' repeated Peter.

On the fourth day, it was very dry and they didn't find any water. Peter walked slowly. He didn't feel very well. Then he sneezed. The bush boy began to laugh again. He remembered Peter's first sneeze. Peter sneezed again.

'You've got a cold, Peter,' said Mary.

'I know,' said Peter through his nose. He sneezed again. He sneezed all day, and his nose was red.

Aboriginals never sneezed and never caught colds. The bush boy didn't understand.

'What's he doing? What's wrong with him?' asked the bush boy. But of course Mary and Peter didn't understand the question.

That evening, Peter didn't help with the fire. He was too tired and too ill. Mary put her arms round him, and in a minute he was asleep. The bush boy cooked food for the two of them. Then he put out the fire. He was happier. The two children walked well, and it was not far now. He found a place to sleep.

But suddenly, he sneezed. He put his hand to his face. It felt hot. That was very strange. Perhaps he was ill too.

In the morning, Peter felt better. He got up and looked for the bush boy. He saw him in the rocks, and went down to him. The bush boy stood near some water. He had a large, round rock in his hands. He looked at Peter and smiled.

'*Yarrawa*!' he said, excited.

Peter looked. There were a lot of fish in the water.

'Is that *yarrawa*?' he asked. There were thousands of little fish. They swam very fast.

'*Yarrawa*,' said the bush boy again.

'But how can you catch them?' asked Peter.

The bush boy smiled again. He threw his rock into the water as hard as he could. The rock hit the water with a loud noise. The water came up round the two boys, and over them too. But on the top of the water Peter saw the fish. Now they didn't move.

'Are they dead?' he asked. But of course they weren't.

The bush boy jumped into the water. He took a lot of the fish and threw them on to the dry rocks. Then he climbed out of the water. He hit the fish on the head with a rock. He gave some fish to Peter, and he carried the other fish. They took them to Mary, and cooked them for breakfast. They couldn't eat them all, so they carried some for their dinner later.

That evening, they sat round the fire and ate *yarrawa*. Then the bush boy suddenly got up and started to dance. He danced round the fire. He danced very fast. Then suddenly, in the middle of his dance, he sneezed. He sneezed again and again. He felt weak and ill, so he sat down. He put his hand to his face, and it was hot and wet. But he also felt very cold, and now he was afraid.

'This is the end,' he thought. 'I'm going to die now.'

Peter and Mary watched the bush boy.

'What's he doing?' asked Peter.

'I don't know,' said Mary. 'It's very strange. Perhaps he caught your cold.'

Later, when it was dark, Peter and Mary slept. But the bush boy stood on the rocks and looked out at the desert again for a long time. The fire was warm, and he tried to sleep near it. But he sneezed often, and he was very cold. He couldn't get warm.

In the morning, he didn't make a fire, and there wasn't any breakfast.

'Mary, is he ill?' asked Peter.

'No, he's not ill,' answered Mary. But she didn't really know.

Peter went to the bush boy. 'Hey, boy, are you OK? Let's go. Adelaide, remember? We have to go to Adelaide.'

The bush boy stood up slowly. Yes, Peter was right. They had to leave. They walked all morning. Nobody said a word. They stopped for lunch, and the bush boy found some eggs. Fourteen big bird's eggs. The children cooked and ate them. The bush boy didn't eat. Then they were thirsty, but there wasn't any water. The bush boy was tired and weak. He didn't move for a long time. Then he got up, and started to walk again.

The bush boy looked out at the desert for a long time.

That night, Peter and Mary found wood for the fire. Next morning, Peter woke first. He walked down the rocks to the river and had a good swim. He climbed back to the others.

'I'm going for a swim too,' said Mary. 'Can you start a fire, Pete?'

'Yes, of course!'

Peter walked to some trees, and began to find wood for the fire. Mary had a long, long swim.

The bush boy woke up alone. He felt very weak.

'I'm going to die,' he thought. 'But first, I have to ask the children for help. It's very important. They're my friends, but they don't understand. So I have to teach them about death in my tribe.'

He heard Mary in the river below, and walked down to her. She was in the water, and she was naked, without her strange clothes. He watched her long hair in the water. It was very beautiful. Suddenly Mary looked up and saw him. She was very afraid. She moved away, and she found a small rock.

'I can throw this at him,' she thought.

'Go away!' she shouted.

The bush boy didn't understand, and he came nearer.

'Stay there! Don't come nearer!'

He saw hate in her eyes.

'She's not a friend,' he thought. 'I can't talk to her. She won't help me. And the boy won't understand. He's too young. So I'll have to die alone.'

Slowly he turned and walked a little way into the desert. He found a sad mugga-wood tree.★

'This is a good place,' he thought. 'I'll die here.'

And only the great red flowers of the mugga-wood tree cried for him.

◆

★ mugga-wood tree: for Aboriginals, the mugga-wood is a sad tree, because its flowers are always wet and red. They say that the tree is crying.

Mary went back to Peter. She started to put out the fire.

'Hey,' said Peter. 'Don't do that! We're going to have breakfast.'

'There isn't any breakfast.'

'What do you mean?'

'Listen, Peter.' She spoke very quietly. 'There isn't any food here. Let's go.'

'What's wrong with you, Mary? Why do you want to go now? The boy will get us some food.'

'Listen, Pete. Please. Let's go. You and me. We'll be OK.'

Peter's mouth fell open. 'We can't leave the boy.'

'He doesn't want to come, Pete. I *know* he doesn't. I asked him.'

'You didn't,' said Peter. 'You can't talk the boy's language!'

'I'm telling you,' she said, 'that he doesn't want to come. I *know*.'

In South Carolina, Peter was never difficult. But now, things were different.

'*I'm* going to ask him,' he said. He ran to the bush boy.

'Pete! Come back,' shouted Mary. But Pete didn't stop. Mary sat down sadly by the fire. After about ten minutes, Peter came back.

'Mary! The boy's ill. Really ill. He's under a tree, and he can't get up.'

'Perhaps he's asleep.'

'No, no, he's not asleep. He's ill! Come and see.'

'No! No!' Mary moved away from Peter. 'No!' she said quietly. 'I'm not going near him.'

The day was long and difficult. Mary sat alone.

'We have to leave now,' she said again and again.

But Peter didn't hear her. He stayed with the bush boy. He took water to him in his hands, but the bush boy didn't drink. There wasn't any food, and the bush boy got weaker and weaker.

'He's really going to die,' thought Peter sadly. 'I'm going to lose my friend.'

31

He took the bush boy's hand. The bush boy said something. Peter couldn't hear, so he put his face near the bush boy's head.

'*Arkooloola!*'

Peter ran and got some water in his hands. But the boy didn't want to drink. He put his hands on Peter's hands.

'Me? No, I don't want a drink,' said Peter.

But the bush boy put his hands on Peter's hands again, and then he sat up. He showed him the hills far away to the south.

'*Arkooloola*,' said the bush boy again. '*Yeemara.*'

'Ah, I understand. Over there, there's food and water. *Arkooloola* and *yeemara*. That's great! Thanks!' Peter took the boy's hand. 'Now you can sleep.'

But then Peter thought of something. He got up and walked to his sister. She looked up.

'How is he?'

'I think he's really dying,' said Peter.

'Oh no! No. No. No.'

Mary put her hands over her face. Peter looked at her. Then he remembered his question.

'Do you think he'll go to heaven, Mary? I mean, he doesn't go to church. So perhaps he can't go to heaven.'

'Is he *really* ill, Pete?'

'Yes. Come quickly. Come and see.'

Mary said nothing. She looked at Peter. Then she looked down at the rocks, and she looked at the hills, far away. Then she said slowly, 'OK. I'll come.'

They walked to the bush boy's tree. She looked into his face.

'You're right, Pete. He's dying. What'll we do?'

She sat down and took the bush boy's head in her hands. She put her hands on his face. The bush boy opened his eyes and looked at her. Then he smiled. Mary suddenly understood a lot of things for the first time.

'I was very stupid,' thought Mary. It was too late, but she knew now. There weren't two different worlds – *his* world, and *her* world. There was *one* world, for everybody.

The bush boy died early in the morning. The desert was asleep. Nothing moved – not the animals, not the plants, not Mary. She was asleep too, next to the bush boy, and her long hair fell over his face.

Chapter 5   Out of the Bush

Mary and Peter made a bed on the ground for the dead boy. They put wood and rocks over him. Pete put some of the red flowers from the mugga-wood tree on the top. When a person died in South Carolina, everybody went to church. There was no church here. But they stayed quietly with the dead boy for a short time. They sat near him, but they said nothing.

Then Peter stood up. He was in charge now.

'Let's go!' he said. '*Kurura!*'

'Where to?'

'Over the mountains!'

'Is that the right way, Pete?' Mary asked.

'Yes, the boy told me. Over the mountains, there's food and water.'

'All right,' she said. 'Let's go.'

They started to walk. They walked carefully, and they found food and water. The bush boy's lessons helped them. They knew the desert now.

That night, they stopped and built a fire. They sat and talked sadly about the bush boy.

'Do you think he's in heaven, Mary?'

'Yes. Yes, he's up there. I think he's watching us. We all live in the same world, Pete. When we die, there's only one place for all of us.'

Pete smiled. He looked up at the sky for a long time.

Next morning, the children left early. They were in the hills now. They climbed and climbed. When they were at the top of one hill, there was always another hill behind it. The journey was difficult, and they didn't find much food. When they found water, it was often very dirty. But the desert was their home now. They, too, could survive there. South Carolina was far, far away.

'Is this the right way,' asked Mary again.

'Yes, yes,' said Peter. 'The boy told me. Over the hills.'

But there were always more hills. That night, they slept in the rocks, but they had no food. Then the next day, after three hours, they came to the last hill. They were at the top!

'Look, Mary! *Yeemara* and *arkooloola*!' said Peter excitedly.

The boy was right. At the bottom of the hill, everything was green. There was food and water below. Hand in hand, the children started to run down the mountain, to the rivers, the trees, and the green plants.

♦

The country was very beautiful. It was wonderful after their difficult life in the desert. There was food everywhere, and a lot of water. There were birds in the trees and fish in the rivers. The plants and the trees had fruit on them. The children were a little afraid of the big, tall, dark trees, but then they began to play in them.

Peter climbed up a tree. 'This is great!' he shouted to Mary, and then she climbed the tree too. They played all day, and they were friends again.

On the third day, they saw a koala in a tree. It was a mother koala with her baby. Pete went up into the tree. He took the baby from the mother and gave it to Mary.

'There now! Play with that!' said Peter.

The mother koala started to make strange sounds. She wanted her baby.

At the bottom of the hill, everything was green.

'Oh Peter! How could you do that! You bad boy!'

She tried to give the baby back to its mother, but it caught her dress. It pulled and pulled. Mary's dress came off and fell to the ground.

'Oh, my dress!' said Mary. She laughed. She felt good now, with no clothes on. She was a different Mary now.

♦

'I never want to leave here,' said Peter on the sixth day.

The children played and played. They swam for hours in beautiful blue water. They forgot Adelaide, and Uncle Keith, and they forgot their old life in South Carolina. Mary sometimes thought of home in Charleston, but not often. They were very, very happy.

On the seventh day, the children found a beautiful wide river. They sat with their feet in the warm water.

'Hey, look over there,' said Peter. 'Smoke! There's a fire.'

'And people!' said Mary.

'Yes, people. How many are there?'

'Three, I think.'

'Let's make a fire too. Then they'll see us.'

'OK.'

They found wood and built a fire. The three people saw the smoke. They ran down to the water, and started to swim across the river to Peter and Mary.

'They're coming, Pete!'

Mary was excited, but also afraid. She didn't have any clothes now. She couldn't say hello without any clothes. Not to white people.

'Do you think they're white, Pete?'

Peter looked carefully. 'No, I think they're black. They're the same as the boy,' he said.

She felt better. They stood near the river, and watched. They saw a family of Aboriginals – a father, a mother and a young girl. And on the father's head, there was a baby. The mother and daughter swam with food and other things on their heads. There was a dog with them too.

They came near, and climbed out of the water. They were friendly, and they smiled at Peter and Mary. The woman gave Mary some food. Peter played with the dog. The black people talked and talked. Mary didn't understand very much. But they talked with their hands too, and she watched carefully.

'Wait a minute,' thought Mary. 'They're telling me something. Is that a house? Are those people? Yes, they're trying to help us.'

'Pete!' she said. 'They know we're lost. They're telling us about houses. About white people. They live over there. But where? Oh, where?'

Then the black man made a map on the ground. He showed her a mountain, a road and a house. He showed her a place for the night. They could sleep there. And he showed her food and water. It was two days' journey. Mary looked at the map and laughed.

'What's funny?' asked Peter.

She showed him the map.

'Look at this map! Why do we use language?' she said.

A little later, the family started to walk to the river.

'I think they want to go now, Pete,' she said.

Peter went to the black man and put out his hand.

'Goodbye!' he said.

The black man smiled and put out his hand too. Mary also said goodbye, and the family started to swim back across the river.

Mary and Peter sat near the river and watched them. Then Peter stood up. He was ready for the journey home.

'Are you coming, Mary?' he asked.

Mary looked round her.

'Oh Pete!'

'I'll always remember this.'

'What 's wrong now, Mary?'

Mary started to cry. 'It's really, really beautiful here!'

'I know,' said Peter. 'I'll always remember this.'

He looked round at everything too. Then he turned to Mary.

'But we have to go, Mary. Let's go home. *Kurura.*'

ACTIVITIES

Introduction and Chapter 1

Before you read

1 What do you know about Australia? Find a book about the country.
   - **a** How big is it?
   - **b** How many people live there?
   - **c** Where are the big cities?
   - **d** How many people are Aboriginal?
   - **e** When did they come to Australia?

2 Read the Introduction, and answer these questions. Find the words in *italics* in your dictionary.
   - **a** What is a Walkabout? How long does a boy have to *survive*? Is he *alone*, or does his family help him?
   - **b** Why is life in the Australian *bush* difficult?
   - **c** Why are two American children *lost*? Where did their plane *crash*? Is it *far* to the city of Adelaide?

3 Answer these questions. Find the words in *italics* in your dictionary.
   - **a** Are *ants* big or small? Are they fish or *insects*?
   - **b** Is a *desert* wet or dry?
   - **c** Is a flower a *plant* or an animal?
   - **d** Can you build a wall or a boat from *rocks*?

After you read

4 Discuss these questions.
   - **a** Is Mary clever? Is she kind?
   - **b** What will be the children's biggest problem in the desert?

5 Work with another student. Have this conversation.

   Student A: You are Mary. Peter is swimming in the middle of the river. You are angry with him.

   Student B: You are Peter. You are not a baby. (But you want her help when you have ants in your trousers!)

Chapters 2–3

Before you read

6 James Vance Marshall wrote this story in the 1950s. Mary's home

is in Charleston, South Carolina. Why is this important in the story? What do you know about life in the south of the USA at this time?

7 What do the words in *italics* mean? Talk about them. Use the words below, and your dictionary.

death   heaven   hill   in charge   sneeze   piece   naked   tribe
boss   ill   without clothes   people   after life   mountain   not all

After you read

8 Discuss these questions.
   a Why is the bush boy naked?
   b How do Peter and Mary understand the bush boy?
   c How does Mary know that the bush boy is friendly?
   d How does the bush boy help Peter and Mary?
   e Why does the bush boy walk into the desert?

9 Mary has two problems. Which are they?
   a The desert is dirty.
   b She is too hot.
   c She feels alone when Peter plays with the bush boy.
   d She doesn't like the bush boy.
   e She thinks that the bush boy can kill them.
   f She thinks that he can't help them.
   g She is afraid of the bush boy because he is a young man.

Chapters 4–5

Before you read

10 What do you think?
   a Will Mary, Peter and the bush boy survive in the desert?
   b Will Mary and Peter find their way home?
   c Will they meet other people?
   d Who will be in charge at the end of the story: the bush boy, Mary or Peter?

11 If you catch a *cold*, how do you feel?

After you read

12 In the story:
   a what changes between Mary and the bush boy?

41

    b what does Mary learn about life?

    c why does the bush boy die?

    d how do things change between Mary and Peter?

13 Discuss the questions.

    a Is this a sad story or a happy story?

    b What did you learn from the story?

Writing

14 Mary arrives in a small town. She telephones Uncle Keith. Write the telephone conversation. Begin:

    Mary: Hello. Is that Uncle Keith?

15 Mary remembers a day from her life in the bush. Write it for her. Begin:

    I woke up early and ...

16 Peter remembers a day in the bush. Write it for him. Begin:

    First I had a swim. Then ...

17 Mary and Peter are in Adelaide now. Write about the bush boy for a newspaper. What are the good things about him and his life? How did he help the American children?